Dear Parents:

Congratulations! Your child is taking the first steps on an exciting journey. The destination? Independent reading!

STEP INTO READING® will help your child get there. The program offers five steps to reading success. Each step includes fun stories and colorful art or photographs. In addition to original fiction and books with favorite characters, there are Step into Reading Non-Fiction Readers, Phonics Readers and Boxed Sets, Sticker Readers, and Comic Readers—a complete literacy program with something to interest every child.

Learning to Read, Step by Step!

Ready to Read   Preschool–Kindergarten
• big type and easy words • rhyme and rhythm • picture clues
For children who know the alphabet and are eager to begin reading.

Reading with Help   Preschool–Grade 1
• basic vocabulary • short sentences • simple stories
For children who recognize familiar words and sound out new words with help.

Reading on Your Own   Grades 1–3
• engaging characters • easy-to-follow plots • popular topics
For children who are ready to read on their own.

Reading Paragraphs   Grades 2–3
• challenging vocabulary • short paragraphs • exciting stories
For newly independent readers who read simple sentences with confidence.

Ready for Chapters   Grades 2–4
• chapters • longer paragraphs • full-color art
For children who want to take the plunge into chapter books but still like colorful pictures.

STEP INTO READING® is designed to give every child a successful reading experience. The grade levels are only guides; children will progress through the steps at their own speed, developing confidence in their reading.

Remember, a lifetime love of reading starts with a single step!

Step into Reading, Random House, and the Random House colophon are registered trademarks of Penguin Random House LLC.

Visit us on the Web!
rhcbooks.com

Educators and librarians, for a variety of teaching tools, visit us at RHTeachersLibrarians.com

ISBN 978-0-7364-4487-3 (trade) — ISBN 978-0-7364-9049-8 (lib. bdg.)
ISBN 978-0-7364-4488-0 (ebook)

Printed in the United States of America

10 9 8 7 6 5 4 3 2 1

DISNEY MOANA 2

The Great Voyage

adapted by Natasha Bouchard

illustrated by the Disney Storybook Art Team

Random House 🏠 New York

Ever since Moana
restored the heart of
Te Fiti, she has been
a living legend on the
island of Motunui.
Storytellers share her
tale as an important part
of the island's history.

The people of Motunui now
honor their voyaging past.
They build new canoes to
sail beyond the reef and
to the horizon.

Moana returns home from
an ocean voyage. She was
exploring other islands,
hoping to find other people.

There is so much more for
Moana to discover. One day, she
hopes to share the entire ocean
with her little sister, Simea.

Moana's ancestors call on her to
find the lost island of Motufetū.
It was once the gathering place
for all of the ocean's people.

The journey to the far sea will
be long and dangerous. Moana
gathers a crew and they set
sail on an epic voyage!

The crew members have never voyaged before. They are not prepared for the challenge.

Moana shows them that
an adventure at sea can be
exciting! She convinces her
crew that there is nothing
better than sailing out on
the vast ocean.

After a few days, Moana
and her crew think they see
the island of Motufetū up ahead.
Moana soon realizes that it is
actually an enemy's ship!

And it's heading straight
toward Moana's canoe!
The Kakamora are preparing
for battle. Moana and her
crew panic!

But the Kakamora are not chasing
Moana's canoe. They are trying
to escape a giant clam!
The massive sea creature
sucks up everything around it.

It is blocking Moana from
her journey to the lost island.
The Kakamora are also searching
for Motufetū. They team up with
Moana to defeat the clam.

Moana prepares to throw a spear at the clam. She thinks it will be easy, but everything goes wrong. Their canoe is in danger of being swallowed by the clam!

At the last minute, the Kakamora chief's son comes to the rescue. Kotu zips onto their canoe and throws a toxin-filled spear at the monster clam.

The clam begins to close.

Moana's canoe and the

Kakamora's ship are about

to be swallowed!

But Kotu cuts the rope to save

the rest of the Kakamora.

Kotu, Moana, and her crew

get sucked into the clam!

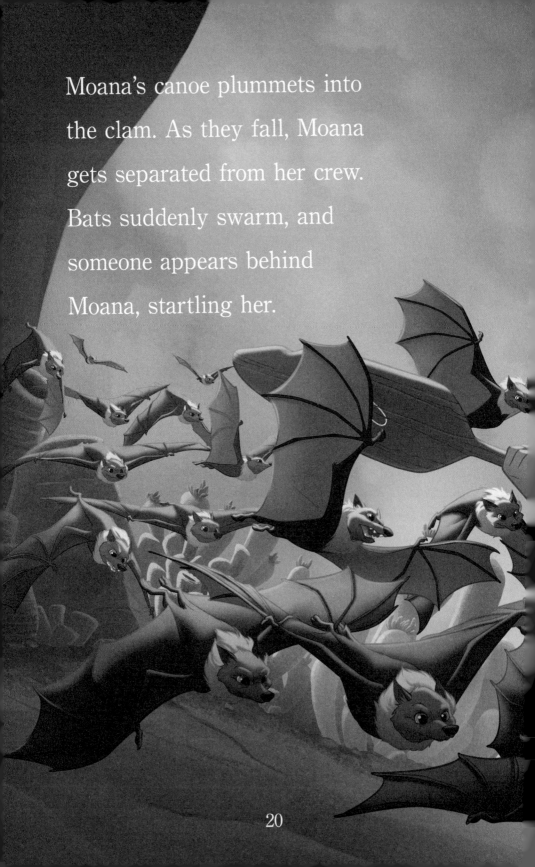

Moana's canoe plummets into the clam. As they fall, Moana gets separated from her crew. Bats suddenly swarm, and someone appears behind Moana, startling her.

It is Matangi, a demigod who offers to help. She tells Moana that to find what she is looking for, she has to get lost. Moana takes her advice and is trapped. Matangi tricked her!

Meanwhile, the crew finds
a familiar demigod tied up.
Matangi trapped Maui, too!
The crew retrieves Maui's
magical hook. He sets himself
free and helps them find Moana.

Soon after they find her, Moana
locates a secret portal. When she
opens it, Moana, Maui, and the
crew are sucked through a tunnel!
They are spit out with their
canoe into the far sea.

Maui warns that the far sea is cursed. The curse can only be broken when a human reaches Motufetū, now at the bottom of the sea. Determined to find the lost island, the crew battles waves that transform into a menacing water monster!

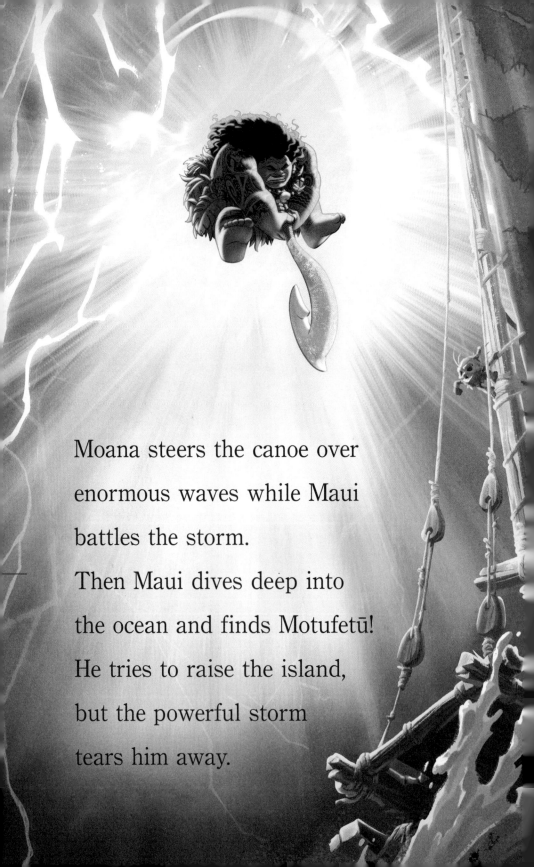

Moana steers the canoe over
enormous waves while Maui
battles the storm.
Then Maui dives deep into
the ocean and finds Motufetū!
He tries to raise the island,
but the powerful storm
tears him away.

Moana dives into the dark waves
and gives in to the unknown.
She reaches Motufetū and
helps Maui raise the island.
The curse is broken at last!
Soon wayfinders from distant
shores arrive to meet Moana.

The wayfinders place tokens from
their home islands on Motufetū.
Moana is proud to reunite
all the people of the ocean.

Moana sets off on new adventures!
Wayfinders from other islands
join her to explore distant lands.